Copyright © 2023 by Matilda Martel

All rights reserved. No part of this book may be reproduced or transmitted in any form, including electronic or mechanical, without written permission from the publisher, except in the case of brief quotations embodied in critical articles or reviews.

This is a work of fiction. Names, characters, businesses, places, events, and incidents are either the products of the author's imagination or used in a fictitious manner. Any resemblance to actual persons, living or dead, or actual events is purely coincidental.

This book is licensed for your personal enjoyment only.

Cover Design by: Love the Cover and Design Rans

Edited by Oopsie Daisy Edits

Proofread by JudyAnnLovesBook

ORPHAN

MATILDA MARTEL

CHAPTER 1
ANNI

"Good morning. I'm here to see Mr. Oliver Warbrick." I listen to the sound of my trembling voice and release a long, audible breath, my rising nerves making it difficult to speak.

The woman behind the tall desk slides her glasses down the bridge of her nose and gives me a once-over, her brows wrinkled with disapproval.

I drop my gaze and stare at the childish red dress I chose to wear and cringe. It was the best I could find in the church thrift shop after the other girls picked it through. My best friend, Edie, swore it was age appropriate for a teenage girl, but I was hoping for something that looked more like eighteen than thirteen. It's too late now to consider alternative options. I'm here, moments from meeting the only man I'll ever love.

"What's your name?" The receptionist turns to look at her monitor, typing furiously as her eyes scan the screen.

I clear my throat and scoot closer to whisper, "Annika Bennett, ma'am."

Her eyes grow wide with recognition, and her expression grows soft. "I'm sorry, sweetheart. You're with the St. Mary's applicants. You should have said something right off the bat." She looks over her shoulder and points to the clock overhead. "There's someone with him now, but you'll get your shot in ten minutes. Would you like some water while you wait?"

I shake my head, my throat too tight to drink anything. "No, thank you. Will you let me know when he's ready? I don't want to miss my turn." I gesture to the row of chairs indicating my intended location and wait for her to reply.

"Of course, dear. I'll let you know when your time comes." She offers a warm smile and soothes my paranoia with a nod.

I amble towards the closest chair and quietly take a seat, hyper-aware of my surroundings and how much I don't fit in. Everything in sight exudes luxury. The chairs aren't the typical cookie-cutter metal with padded polyester seats. They're tufted leather and polished wood wingback armchairs decorated with brass flourishes. The plants are real, the carpets are Persian, and the art-deco lighting looks like it cost a fortune. The more I look, the more out of place I feel.

We're from two different worlds. He's everything, and I'm nothing. But I can make myself into something. I can prove I'm worthy of his love and work hard to become the woman he needs. It's easier to slink away and take the path of least resistance. That's not me. As much as I want to run away, I won't let my past prevent me from walking through those doors and facing my destiny head-on.

I know I sound crazy and cringeworthy. But he's all I have. I don't remember my parents. What little family remained turned me away when I was still in diapers. The few foster parents who took me in treated me like an inconvenience. Shortly after I turned eleven, the state of New York stopped trying to find me a home and tucked me away at St. Mary's—out of sight and out of mind. That's when I first came across a photo of a dashing Oliver Warbrick, casually dressed at the helm of a 200-foot yacht. His chiseled face, deep brown eyes, salt-and-pepper hair, and the obvious muscular physique hidden beneath a tight pullover sweater drew me in like the gravitational pull of a black hole and sent me galloping into puberty.

I fell head over heels in love with a man I'd never met. Oliver became more than the man of my dreams—he was the daddy I never had. Someone who would make me feel wanted, loved, cherished, and always keep me safe. Oliver owns me—heart and soul. He's all I think about. All I dream about. For seven years, I've stalked him online, read his books, and devoured every article I could find. I've clipped photos and taped them to a scrapbook I keep tucked away beneath my mattress. Every night before bed, I pore through it and fantasize about the day I'll stand before him, face to face, and tell him what he means to me. It's my prized possession and the only thing that brings me comfort as I take my first steps into adulthood and a dim future full of uncertainties.

An orphan can only be an orphan until they turn eighteen. Unfortunately for me, that milestone came and went last month. I've overstayed my welcome at St. Mary's Home for Girls and tried in vain to find alternate living arrangements. I'm not homeless—not yet. But an eighteen-year-old girl with no education or employment experience can't work enough hours to pay rent, utilities, and groceries in New York.

College is my only hope. I had the grades to get into NYU but needed more money to pay tuition, fees, and half a dormitory room to keep me off the streets. Then Oliver appeared like a knight in shining armor to save the day. Not him in person, of course. A man with his responsibilities has too much on his plate to traipse across town to Lower Manhattan and visit an aging orphanage, the last refuge for girls who were never placed in individual foster homes.

Last week he sent his assistant, Grace Bellamy, to St. Mary's for a lengthy presentation for girls interested in continuing their education after high school. Only three of us qualified this year, but she assured us Mr. Warbrick's generosity would continue for the foreseeable future. Her news brought a flicker of hope into my bleak world. This is my chance to make something of myself and prove I'm worthy of a man like Oliver.

He's a wealthy man, one of the richest in Manhattan, and he deserves a woman who can offer him more than a pretty face and a warm bed. I know there's a slim chance of impressing him, but I have to try. I won't squander this once-in-a-lifetime opportunity. With hard work, dedication, and luck, I'll finish school in three and a half years, then apply to work with Warbrick Industries. It might take years, but one day, I'll pass him in a crowded executive hallway and say hello. We'll share a tender moment, and somehow, someway, he'll see the love in my eyes and know fate brought us together.

That was my plan before Grace Bellamy invited all three finalists to meet Oliver Warbrick in person. It was too good to be true, and my greatest nightmare rolled into one. I'm not ready to meet him. I'm an orphan with zero sophistication and life experience—a nobody who wears secondhand clothes and worn-out shoes. He'll take one look at me and either laugh or take pity on my pathetic, poverty-stricken soul.

I remove a tissue from my purse and dab the corner of my eyes. No matter what happens, I won't cry. I never expected to get this far or come so close, and I must keep my eyes on the prize. The most important thing is snagging that scholarship money and saving myself from a life of odd jobs and women's shelters. Men, even one as perfect as Oliver Warbrick, can wait. If all goes well, we'll meet again and maybe even share a laugh about this incredibly awkward day.

Stranger things have happened. Not to me. Nothing's

happened to me. But it will. If I can remain focused on the task at hand and not the big, beautiful man sitting inside that office, everything might turn out as fate intended.

"Annika Bennett?" A woman's voice and the soft clatter of heels bring me back from the endless abyss of my vivid imagination, and draw my attention toward the open door.

I jump to my feet and embarrass myself by raising my hand. "Yes! I'm Annika!"

"I know, dear." The receptionist smiles and stands to one side, allowing me to pass into the executive lobby. "Mr. Warbrick is ready for you." She pats my shoulder and then points to the French doors at the end of the hallway. "Good luck."

I nod and give her a thumbs-up that makes me shrink with shame. It's too late to learn social graces and sophistication. The man of my dreams holds my future in the palm of his hands, and it's up to me to persuade him to give me a chance. If I don't rein in my anxiety, I may explode as soon as I say hello.

The receptionist offers a nudge of encouragement that gets my feet moving forward. With small, careful, calculated steps, I reach his door and stare longingly at the placard on the wall —Oliver A. Warbrick, Chief Executive Officer.

I'm here, and he's in there. Only a door separates us.

I lift my fist and give the wood a light tap. Here goes nothing.

CHAPTER 2
OLIVER

"You have one final candidate, and she's my favorite. Don't let that influence your decision. But don't check out before you've had a chance to consider her. She's lovely and has the highest GPA of the three." Grace's chirpy voice interrupts my bored daze, and my mind quickly spins to recover. I glance at the screen, click the tab, and scan the names on my calendar. Annika Bennett? Why does that name feel familiar? I'm sure I've never heard it before, but there's something about the way it rolls off my tongue.

Annika Bennett.

"She's got the grades. What else makes her so special? I didn't graduate with a 4.0, and look where I am today." I spread my arms like a king surveying his kingdom and smirk, expecting her to come back with a doozie.

Grace matches my sarcasm and mocks me, spinning in circles with her arms extended over her head. "What was I thinking? I'm sure if Annika Bennett inherited your father's billions, she too could have thrown caution to the wind and slacked off in school."

My smile disappears in a flash. "He didn't leave me

billions, jerk. He left me millions that I turned into billions. Give me an ounce of credit."

"Pardon me, Oliver Twist. I forgot all about your humble beginnings." She rolls her eyes and drops a folder on my desk. "Here's her application and essay. She'll bring an extra copy, but you should take a moment to read through it. She's a double orphan, survived the system relatively unscathed, and in less than a week, they'll kick her out of the only stable home she's ever known. Not only will she have zero people cheering for her when she walks across the stage for her high school graduation, but she'll also have nowhere to go when it's over. No one gave this girl a silver spoon. Your help will change the course of her life and break the horrible cycle of poverty that awaits her."

My face heats with embarrassment. I need to learn when to shut my mouth. "Sorry I made a joke about it. Send her in."

Grace steps backward and retreats toward the door. "Behave yourself, Oliver. If you don't like her, I'll understand, but keep an open mind, and please, don't ogle her."

"Ogle her? For fuck's sake, she's eighteen years old. She's practically a fetus. I can't believe you'd even suggest such..." A light tap and slow creak make my head snap towards the door. I squint and lift my hand to my forehead, shielding my eyes from the sunlight pouring in through the floor-to-ceiling windows. The sight catches me by surprise, and I stare with intent as a pair of tiny feet tiptoe over the threshold.

She's wearing white socks and black Mary Jane flats, an unusual choice that piques my curiosity and spikes my discomfort. My gaze travels helplessly along the path of a sun-kissed calf to the divine slope of a shapely thigh peeking past her pleated hem.

I shake my head, trying to rid my brain of inappropriate thoughts. I'm forty, with a firm grasp on morality, and she's a high school senior. This is beyond unsuitable. It's atrocious.

"Mr. Warbrick? Thank you for seeing me today. My name is Anni, Annika Bennett, and I'm a resident of St. Mary's Home. The receptionist said you were ready for me." She slinks into my office with a sheepish gait, destroying my willpower with a single glance. My breath catches, and I stand to greet the living embodiment of forbidden temptation dressed in a fire-engine-red dress.

I'm speechless. Unbearably hard, and speechless.

Grace clears her throat to break the awkward silence coming from my side of the room. "I'm so glad you made it, Annika. I just told Mr. Warbrick about your impressive record at Cathedral High School."

"Annika Bennett?" I repeat her name, incapable of forming words on my own. She's beautiful. Breathtaking. A blue-eyed angel sent to test my dark, depraved soul. My thundering heart makes me fight for breath, my chest rising and falling as beads of sweat trickle down my spine. I feel like Job, chosen by God to prove his loyalty in the face of ultimate temptation. Am I so weak? No, I refuse to fall for the allure of the forbidden. I'm stronger than this.

"Please, come in and take a seat," I stammer, staring dumbfounded as she gathers her auburn hair on one shoulder, and her luminous eyes widen with surprise. I drink her in, ravishing every inch of exposed skin with my filthy gaze. Shame devours me, but I can't tear my eyes away. I'm a glutton who wants to feast on every curve and plane of her delectable body.

She saunters forward, shielding her breasts with a rainbow-striped folder clutched tightly to her chest. Before she sits, she lifts the hem of her dress, revealing the supple skin of her inner thigh, and I nearly fly over my desk to get a better look. I'm a wicked man.

Annika bows her head, thumbs through her folder, and selects two sheets of paper she hands over in a rush. I steady my hand and reach across the desk to take it from her delicate fingers.

"Is this your essay?" I swallow hard and bow my head to examine it, my eyes moving left to right at a panicked pace. I should have taken Grace's advice and read it in advance because I want to know everything there is to know about the tiny girl who just blew up my world.

Random words flash before me. Orphan. Foster care. Abandoned by relatives. The word eighteen flies off the page and fights to slap some sense into my lust-addled brain. She's too young for me, but the more I sit in her company, the less it matters. It's loathsome and unethical but technically not illegal.

"It says here that you'd like to study public relations. Can you tell me more about your interest in that field?" I point to the pages, hoping to spend more time with her by prolonging the interview. If necessary, I'll keep this up until the end of the day.

"Yes, of course." She scoots her ass to the edge of her seat, excitedly gesturing as she speaks. "I plan to major in Public Relations with a minor in Mass Communications. Every major corporation needs a good PR person who will represent the company and safeguard its reputation with the media. If I'm awarded the Warbrick Fellowship, I will, of course, seek employment here first and hopefully become an asset to your company."

The prospect of having her here, under my loving tutelage, makes my wicked heart stammer. I need a new publicist, and I bet she'd be good at it. Every man she meets will fall head over heels in love, which is a thought that doesn't sit right with my soul. I can already sense those fucking vultures circling, hoping to take her for themselves... over my dead, bloated corpse.

"Mr. Warbrick, this scholarship has the potential to change my life. If I'm selected as this year's recipient, I promise I won't let you down. I'll work hard and dedicate myself to my studies." She straightens her posture, adjusting her white collar and wiggling her bottom on the seat of an oversized chair. She's so short her feet don't touch the ground. She's half my size. A petite and bite-sized morsel to ritually consume until my dying breath. The reprehensible thought and a shudder pass through me. The thought of having her beneath me makes me harder than a slab of tungsten steel.

My breath stalls, and my eyes hood like a predator laser-focused on its prey. There's so much I don't know about the girl sitting in front of me. A two-thousand-word essay, double-spaced with wide margins, is nothing more than a tiny glimpse into her world. I need to know more. I want to know everything there is to learn and then spend the next fifty years helping her write the rest.

"I like what I see—I mean hear." The truth emerges despite my pathetic attempt to save face.

Grace, still idling in the corner of the room with a front-row seat to my descent into madness, injects herself into the conversation. "We'll have the final decision by Monday morning. If you want to leave any extra information or documents with us, I'll take them now."

I tense, my gaze narrowing with annoyance as my trusty assistant attempts to cockblock me.

"Why don't you join me for lunch?" The words fly out of my mouth before I can think long and hard about the consequences of my actions. It's the wrong course, a treacherous road that will twist me into an unrecognizable fiend with no soul or conscience. But would that be so bad? Doesn't happiness count for anything?

Annika's bee-stung lips part with surprise. "I don't understand. Is this part of the interview?" Her confusion offers an escape, but I ignore the angel on my shoulder and give in to the demon lurking deep within. It won't do any good anyway. The moment she leaves, I'll come to my senses and chase her into the street.

"This is the inaugural year for Warbrick Fellowship, and I'd like to ensure you're as ambitious as you claim. We should share a meal and talk about your future. I'd love to learn more about you." I push down the growl vibrating in my chest and slip her cherry-scented essay into my top desk drawer for safekeeping.

"Yes, that sounds wonderful. I'd love to discuss the possibility of internships. I've got plans to work at a coffee shop kitty-corner to school, but I'd much rather gain practical experience here." She clasps her hands, bouncing with enthusiasm.

My brow creases with concern. As much as I want to believe she's here for a reason, that we're two souls drawn to one another like moths to a raging bonfire, she may not be on the same page. After all, she didn't come here for me. She came here for a scholarship. And I'm the dirty old man holding all the cards, practically blackmailing her into sharing a meal.

This is beneath me.

But so is everything else I plan to do to this little girl.

"Lunch? Should we go to lunch? I've got a meeting at noon, but we can order in if you like." Undoubtedly horrified by my behavior, Grace invites herself to our private meeting.

I discreetly angle my head and shoot daggers into her heart. "We don't need a chaperone, Grace. Attend your meeting, and I'll update you when I return."

Annika's big blue eyes lock on mine as a rising flush colors her cheeks bright pink. She nods her head and offers a nearly imperceptible grin. "I could eat."

"Good girl, I mean, brilliant. Let's go."

CHAPTER 3
ANNI

I can't breathe.

I stare through the tinted window of a black Rolls Royce Phantom, the most luxurious car I've ever seen, much less sat in, charging through midtown traffic toward his favorite restaurant. It's difficult to be alone with him in such a small compartment. He's so much bigger than me. His broad chest, massive arms, thick thighs, and long legs occupy most of the backseat. Every breath he takes steals the air from my lungs. The scent of cologne surrounds me and kindles a fire that's never been lit. A part of me wants to jump out at the next light before I cave to my baser needs, jump on his lap and profess my undying love. But my heart prevents me from moving. I don't want to leave his side. Ever.

On our way downstairs, he made small talk about school and the formal expectations of the fellowship I'm still unsure I've won. I listened intently, hoping he's extended our meeting to give me good news, but I may be wrong. There's something else at play. I'm not good at detecting flirtation or the subtle advances of men, but I sense an undercurrent of naughtiness in his stare.

I hope I'm not wrong.

"Do you like Italian food? My mother was Italian. Once a week, she'd kick the cooks out of the kitchen and make one of my grandmother's dishes, passed down for generations. It's one of my favorite memories of her…" He freezes, like he's lost his train of thought, and sighs. "I don't know why I shared that with you. But I genuinely hope you enjoy the cuisine."

I place my hand over my belly and try in vain to settle the swarm of butterflies that took flight the moment he spoke. He slides an inch closer and lifts my chin with one thick index finger, tilting my head until our eyes meet in a heated gaze that takes my breath away. His appraisal makes me shudder. I straighten my back and push my breasts out, proud to be under his watchful eye, ready for assessment, and so eager to please him.

"I hope I don't make you uncomfortable." The pitch of his voice descends into a gravelly rasp so deep it vibrates into my prickled skin.

"I'm glad… you told me," I stammer, too overcome by his proximity to confess how much more I want to know.

"Are you?" He moves closer and places his hand over mine, covering it entirely under his warm palm. "There will be time for that later. Right now, I want to hear about you— your thoughts, hopes, and dreams. Tell me how I can make them a reality."

My mind spins. Is he coming on to me? Is this flirting?

"My dreams? Mr. Warbrick… I'd like to go to college. I'd like to make something of myself." My throat tightens, but I manage to squeak out the words, hoping to understand where this is going. A slight smile touches his lips, and I feel my cheeks heat under his soulful gaze.

"Please, call me Oliver. Do you prefer Annika or Anni?" His silver tenor feels like a potent drug, lulling me into bliss.

I shake my head, then realize my mistake and nod. "It

doesn't matter. I'll answer to both." I'll answer whenever he calls, if only to be in his masculine presence once more.

"May I call you Anni? You look like an Anni. It's sweet and fresh, just like you." He lifts my hand to his lips, and the blush on my cheeks intensifies.

My heart gallops like a thoroughbred taking a victory lap at the Kentucky Derby, and my throbbing pulse steals my breath. His closeness, scent, and gaze make my nipples harden to stiff peaks, tingling against the cotton fabric of the only bra I own. I wish I could have bought something sexy to wear. This dress and the childish lingerie underneath do nothing to enhance my sex appeal.

"You can call me whatever you like," I say, uncomfortably aware of my own inadequacies in the presence of such divine perfection.

"We're here, Anni." His attention shifts to the window, breaking the spell and releasing me from his hypnotic gaze. The door next to me suddenly opens, and I realize we've stopped moving. I offer the driver my hand to help me out of the car, but Oliver pulls me to him, places my behind on his lap, and lifts me from the backseat to the curb. Stunned by the gesture, I glance over my shoulder and find his gorgeous face twisted by a furious expression. His anger is not directed at me but solely focused on his driver.

"Don't let that happen again," he barks at the thin man dressed in a black suit and driving cap.

The driver nods and offers a quick apology, but everything happens so fast, I don't understand what's transpired.

"Is this it?" I point to a building that looks more like double brownstone, intrigued that something like this exists. "It's lovely."

"It is, but you haven't seen anything yet." He takes my hand, threading his fingers in mine as he leads me to the end of the block. The restaurant spills onto the side street, and the entrance is flanked by tall trees and manicured hedges, each decorated with twinkling white lights clearly visible in the light of day.

The hostess sitting behind an old-fashioned podium recognizes Oliver from a distance and jumps off her stool, approaching us with two menus in hand. "Mr. Warbrick, your secretary called ahead and reserved your favorite table. If you would please follow me..."

Oliver lifts his hand, halting her in her tracks. "Do you have anything more private? Preferably a booth where we can sit side by side."

Her eyes narrow, and her mouth spreads into a thin-lipped smile. She drops her gaze, examining me from head to toe and probably wondering why a man like him would want to sit next to someone in such a shabby dress. I instinctively tighten my grip on Oliver's hand and slip behind him like a child seeking comfort from a loving parent. It's an unfamiliar feeling. In all my eighteen years, I've never had anyone I could rely on or trust, but there's something about Oliver's gentle touch that makes me feel safe.

Sensing my discomfort, he trails his thumb against the back of my hand, humming softly as we walk between the long rows of bustling tables, where wide-eyed stares greet us every step of the way.

"Why are they staring?" I whisper, wondering if I look as bad as I feel.

Oliver helps me onto the plush leather of a half-circle booth, hidden from prying eyes by a row of fake cypress trees. I slide in, bouncing on my ass until I reach the opposite end, seemingly much to his chagrin.

"Come back here, little girl." He pats the space next to him, and I bounce back, landing a few inches away, my thigh almost grazing his. "They're not staring at us. They're staring at you, sweetheart. And I can't say I blame them."

My heart races at double speed. My mouth dries in record time. "Me? Why me?"

Did he just call me sweetheart?

What's happening? Where am I? Am I dreaming?

"Because you are undoubtedly the prettiest girl they've ever seen, and they're not used to seeing me in the company of women, particularly one as young as you. I bet they're wondering if you're my long-lost daughter." His sarcastic smile puts me at ease, but his words assure me I've read him wrong. I'm too young for him—an inappropriate choice for a man like him.

My heart wants so much more than friendship, but if this is all he's offering, I'll take whatever I can get—for now.

Beggars can't be choosers.

CHAPTER 4
OLIVER

I f hell exists, I'm about to earn a first-class ticket there.

Annika Bennett is an eighteen-year-old orphan whose life is teetering on the verge of collapse. I lose nothing by helping her. My bank account earns more interest in a single day than the money I'd spend investing in her future. With my financial assistance, she'll become an independent, self-sufficient woman capable of making her own decisions about the direction of her life.

But is that really what I want?

I'm a man of considerable means with houses all over the world and no one at home to, care for, or love. Money attracts the wrong kind of people into my life, and I've learned to keep my distance, guard my heart, and avoid anything deeper than a few casual friendships. I have one younger brother, a ne'er do well named Phillip who only emerges from his drug-fueled jet-setting life to ask me for money. As soon as our parents passed, he had no interest in maintaining a relationship. Grace is my closest friend because I pay her generously to be at my beck and call. What kind of life is that? It's dull and empty, but I've never cared enough to do anything about it.

It's strange to admit at the ripe old age of forty, but I never imagined building a family of my own. And now, it's the only thing on my mind.

"Do you know when you'll make a decision about the fellowship?" She ducks her head to sip a soda from a straw.

I watch, hot and bothered, salivating like a bloodhound at the sight of her puckered, plump lips wrapped tightly around the red-and-white straw. My cock throbs against my thigh, and I shift in my seat, struggling to hide my tented trousers from her innocent eyes. She's worried about school, and I'm preoccupied with useless fantasies.

"Let me ease your mind, Anni. I should have said this from the start. You are officially the first recipient of the Warbrick Fellowship. The foundation will cover all tuition and fees you incur for the next four years, or five if you need extra time to complete your studies." I babble a mile a minute, then exhale loudly, relieved I got that part out of the way. "I don't want you to feel obligated to stay here if I make you uncomfortable. I'm sure there are plenty of places you'd rather be." I cringe as I speak, fearing I sound manipulative and pitiful. If she stays, I don't want it to be an act of pure obligation.

She claps her hands in a frenzied display of gratitude, then freezes with mortification. Clearing her throat, she straightens her back and reclines into the leather seat, patting her tummy like she's full. We're still only halfway through appetizers. It's too soon to call it a day. "Thank you so much, Mr. Warbrick. I mean Oliver. You don't know what this means to me. Will the fellowship be enough to cover my dormitory? I'm afraid I've already worn out my welcome at St. Mary's, and the woman at NYU told me I can move in early if I start summer classes. It doesn't have to be much. I plan to share a room with another girl." Her big eyes widen with hope and gratitude, reeling me in like a fish on a hook.

I nod, then take a swig of wine, inhaling half in one gulp.

"Of course, it includes room and board. Don't concern your-self with costs. I'll speak to someone from Campus Living and secure you a private room. I don't want you sharing such a small space. You deserve privacy."

"Privacy?" She blinks rapidly, fluttering her lashes with disbelief. "I've never had a room all to myself. In the home, there are four girls in every room."

My heart aches to give her more. A private room? This beautiful girl deserves a castle. I was given every advantage imaginable in life, coddled and pampered by my parents, nannies, and teachers. When your father can buy and sell anyone he wants, he ensures his children get the best life has to offer. I've been the center of attention since birth, but I've never made someone else feel like my world revolves around them. Maybe this is what's missing in my life—someone to dote on. After all, she's endured, Anni deserves to be spoiled rotten. "It's the very least I can do. You should have a quiet space to study."

A bright red flush explodes on her pale cheeks. "Thank you. That's incredibly considerate of you. And I promise I won't let you down. I hope we'll meet again after I finish my studies and apply to work for you." She smiles wide, her naïveté on full display.

Does she really think she can get rid of me so easily?

"I'll save a spot just for you." The words come out like a promise—one I intend to keep. But there's no way I'll step aside and leave our future to chance. I plan to lurk nearby every step of the way. Even if I need to keep to the shadows to do it. Someone as lovely as her needs twenty-four-hour protection from the twenty-somethings roaming campus, eager to show her a good time. That's not fucking happening. They wouldn't know the first thing about taking care of her needs.

That's a job for me.

"Why are you being so nice to me?" Her eyes flood with

unshed tears, and she lifts her hands to cover her hot cheeks. "You asked me if I felt obligated to stay, and the answer is no. We've only just met, and you've treated me better and done more for me than anyone I've ever known."

Her tiny sniffle makes my heart break in two, and her melancholy voice makes me want to punish anyone and everyone who ever let her down. If only she knew my intentions, maybe she'd feel differently. But that can't be helped. Whether she accepts me or not, I'll take care of this little girl and give her the life she deserves.

CHAPTER 5
OLIVER

"You cad. You are a horrible, horrible man. Your behavior is tantamount to grooming. Is this who you are? A decade into this job, I'm only now learning that I work for a pervert. Un-freaking-believable." Grace storms into my office without warning and scolds me like an unruly toddler.

This is the first time we've spoken since Friday when I ditched my afternoon to spend it with Annika. There was nothing salacious about our time together, but that didn't stop Grace from blowing up my phone with random questions and accusations to get to the bottom of my interest.

Needless to say, I have no intention of sharing my plans with anyone but Anni. They're private. Untoward. And still in motion.

"You've only worked here eight years, liar." I correct her math and return to my work. On top of my regularly scheduled duties, I have a long list of people to call and tasks to do before I see Anni tomorrow afternoon. I need to be prepared.

Grace's angry scowl transforms into a shit-eating smirk. "I see. So you don't deny your perversions, just my tenure at

Warbrick Industries. Figures. And for your information, I applied here years before you finally hired me, so I have put in a decade of work. But now I think I regret it. How was I supposed to know what kind of man lay underneath your stuffy persona?"

"Enough. Nothing happened. We discussed school and future job opportunities. Annika's a lovely person and needs a father figure in her life. And although I'm not exactly father material, I'd like to think I have something to offer," I ramble, unconvinced by my nonsense.

"Father figure?" Grace offers a justifiable glower, and I change trajectories, still unwilling to admit the truth. Does my behavior disgust me? Slightly. These are uncharted waters, but I've always been a bit of an adventurer.

"How often do you criticize how out of touch I am with ordinary people? Listening to her talk about one tragic situation after another made me realize how fortunate I am, and how much I take my advantages for granted. It warms my heart to help someone who's been dealt a crappy hand in life. Why can't you give me the benefit of the doubt?" I realize I may have to eat my words, but for now, it's best to keep my plans under wrap.

She'll never understand. She can't. Grace married her high school sweetheart. Love landed on her lap before she was old enough to appreciate its rarity.

She folds her arms over her chest and taps her stiletto on the hardwood floor like an angry woodpecker. Her furious expression turns haughty, a visual aid to remind me which one of us has the superior morality. Nothing she could say would make me feel lower than I already do, nor will it make me change my mind. Some unworthy bastard will eventually snag that girl—so it might as well be me.

"I know what you're going to say." I hold out my palm, hoping to prevent the waves of fury from crashing down on me.

"Do you?" Her arms flail briefly before she quickly regains her composure and settles her clenched fists at her waist. "Because I'm speechless."

"You don't sound speechless." I frown, annoyed she'd try to dissuade me.

Grace paces, head bowed and arms swinging like she's getting ready for a fight. She chews her nails, stares at the ceiling like she's cursing the heavens, then gives me the side-eye. "She's eighteen and vulnerable. No one's ever shown her any love. Despite all the horrible circumstances she's faced in her short life, she beat the odds and is standing on the precipice of a much better life. If you swoop in like a knight in shining armor, indulge your sick fantasies, and then leave her —like you always leave women—I fear you'll break her."

I try to interrupt her, but she silences me with a glare.

"I won't presume to understand what you feel because I know you're not a bad person, but I have my suspicions it's far less honorable than you've fooled yourself into believing. You probably think you're sincerely enamored, and maybe you are, but you'll soon realize it isn't real. And when you do, she won't be prepared to handle the aftermath. You'll undo all her hard work for your own selfish reasons, and when that happens, you'll give me no choice but to—" She stops mid-threat and points an accusing finger. "You'll give me no choice but to murder you in your sleep and make it look like an accident."

My jaw drops. "Excuse me?"

Her voice hardens ruthlessly. "You heard me, Oliver Alexander Warbrick. I did not bring that girl into your office to pimp her out. She is bright and beautiful with a head full of dreams. It isn't easy navigating the treacherous waters of the American Foster Care System without emerging bitter and scarred. But she managed to endure years of trauma, and with a good heart and a ton of gumption, to build an escape plan. If you destroy her, so help me, God, I will kill you. So, stop pretending you're not smitten and promise me you will not ruin her life."

I shake my head, stunned by her words and slightly moved by her passion for protecting a woman so dear to me. There's no need to protect Annika from me. I may have sordid designs for her ripe, eighteen-year-old body, but my intentions are still honorable.

"It's not what you think, Grace. I like her. I want to help her. Yes, I find her incredibly attractive, which boggles my mind because I know damn well she's far too young for me. But right now, I'd genuinely like to give her a good start and set her up for success." That sounds entirely plausible. Shady but plausible.

She squints, scrutinizing me from across the room. "Are you seeing her again?"

"I am, and it isn't open for discussion. On Friday, she confided that she may not attend her high school graduation because it felt strange to celebrate alone. I told her I would be there with bells on. I've secured a full row of seats and recruited the interns to attend in exchange for new furniture in their dedicated lounge. All they need to do is dress up and cheer when they call her name. They're calling it a win."

"That's kind...of sweet," she stammers, unwilling to praise me.

"I have my moments." I scribble a few lines on a notepad and tear off the paper, handing it over with a pronounced scowl. "She needs new clothes, something nice for her gradu- ation, and casual clothes for school. Take my credit card and buy her luggage as well. I don't want her to be singled out by bullies and mean girls when she moves her belongings in grocery bags."

She balks, crumples the note, and pretends to laugh. "And why are you telling me? I'm not a personal shopper. Take her shopping like a good sugar daddy and allow me to get back to work."

Thinking she won, Grace tosses the note in my face, does an about-face, and marches out of my office with a victorious grin.

That was much easier than I expected.

CHAPTER 6
ANNI

"Is everything okay? Do I have to bust down the door and haul you out, little girl?" Oliver's patience grows thin.

I fasten the last button on the ridiculously expensive dress he selected after I refused to look further than the clearance rack, and adjust the bodice into place. It's a light-blue, baby-doll dress with flutter sleeves and a plunging bow back. It's by far the prettiest thing I've ever worn and might be the first new dress I've ever owned.

When Oliver suggested new clothes, I assumed he was joking. What man enjoys hanging out at the mall? I should have known he had something more extravagant in mind.

As soon as I hopped into his car, he made a beeline for Fifth Avenue, promising me he only wanted to ensure I had a nice graduation dress. He suspected I was still considering ditching the ceremony and wanted to ensure I wouldn't skip out on such a momentous event. Within the first half hour, I realized he was lying to prevent an argument. Three hours in, we have a trunk full of bags, none containing the item we came to buy.

His generosity embarrasses me, but I'd be lying if I said his attention didn't make me feel like a princess. No one has ever taken me shopping. Orphans get hand-me-downs or ill-fitting, old-fashioned thrift shop clothes. Foster families never wasted good money on me. Whatever money they collected from the State of New York went to their real children, and I was told I should consider myself lucky to have a roof over my head. Things grew slightly better when I arrived at St. Mary's. We wore cookie-cutter school uniforms, each one unmistakable from the other. Except on those rare occasions like picture day, when someone from school was the original owner and made everyone know my shabby dress used to be hers. I never realized how wonderful it would feel to have something brand new.

"I'll be out in a second." I stare into the mirror, twirling left and right, inspecting every angle to ensure it isn't too short. Nuns might frown at the hemline, but I think the graduation gown will keep everything covered throughout the ceremony. I smooth my hands over the material and fixate on the tight bodice, pushing my breasts together. I've never experienced so much lift or seen the twins in this light. It doesn't feel indecent, but will Oliver think I'm trying too hard? Will people from school think I'm immodest?

I place my hand over my racing heart, conscious of how my chest rises and falls with every labored breath. Two centimeters of cleavage emerge past the neckline, and I consider changing dresses, fearing the headmaster will call me a tramp and deny me my diploma. But how will I find another dress that looks this nice?

Oliver taps the door to get my attention. "It's been more than a second. Do you want me to find something else for you? It's your graduation day—a once in a lifetime event. If you don't love it, choose something else."

My heart swells with love for a man who thinks of me as a little girl. He's kind and thoughtful, unlike anyone I've ever known, and so much nicer than I expected. I'm probably his good deed for the week. I only wish I hadn't allowed myself to get attached to him so soon. He changed my life for the better, and I'll never forget him for giving me a chance to build a better life. Next week, when he's moved on to his next project, I'll be getting ready for my first summer session at college. There won't be any time to pine for Oliver Warbrick.

Live in the moment, Anni. It's the only thing that's guaranteed.

I reach for the knob, and my sweaty hand almost slips off the brass. He's an inch away, waiting to appraise me, anxious to see me. I know he's only being nice, but this feels close and intimate. His attention makes my mind spin with thoughts of naughty things that make me blush. I shouldn't have put so much thought into his kindness. But I can't help myself. My nerves are short, and my need to confess becomes harder to suppress every second we're together. I rub my palm against my socks, the only fabric available, then open the door.

"You look stunning. This is the best one by far." Oliver greets me with a smile, his green eyes cataloging every inch of my body. He steps back to gain a better view and twirls his finger, encouraging me to show him the rest. I do as he asks but instinctively adjust the collar and tug the hem, always erring toward modesty. Eight years of Catholic school will do that to you.

"You're a young, beautiful woman," he rasps, his jaw tightening through clipped words. The huskiness of his deep voice lingers in the air, prickling my skin and urging me to confess how much he means to me. "You shouldn't be afraid to show off a little skin."

The strange look in his eyes makes me shiver. I hug my chest, rubbing the gooseflesh spreading across my skin. Does he like what he sees?

"Are you sure it isn't too expensive? You've been so gener-ous. I don't want you to think I'm taking advantage of you."

He frowns, shaking his head as he gestures to the saleswoman idling nearby. "I enjoy taking care of you, Anni. It makes me happy."

"It does?" I mutter hastily, unsure what he means but enthralled with every word. His care is incomparable. His attention is divine. I only wish we could stay like this forever.

"Don't you want to make me happy, too?" He smirks, then turns to the saleswoman and surrenders his credit card.

Happy? If he only knew what I'd do to make him happy.

CHAPTER 7
OLIVER

"This photo was taken at dinner. I treated Anni and the interns to dinner at Toussaint's, and we closed the place down. Those kids really know how to run up a bar tab, but it was worth it. It was more fun than I've had in years." I scroll through my phone and show Grace the highlights from Friday night.

"Toussaint's? You could do better than that, cheapskate," she scolds but keeps her eyes glued to the screen, swiping down as we walk back toward my office. "You did a lovely thing, Oliver. I'm sure she'll remember this night for years. Now I regret not going."

"Annika chose the restaurant, not me. She told me it has a theater background and she's always wanted to see the caricatures of famous actors on the wall. Besides a few photographs, the only memory she has of her real family is a cigar box filled with Playbill booklets her mother collected before she was born. Apparently, she loved musical theater and opera. She's never had the means to attend a Broadway play, so she thought this place was as close as she could get to having her mom present." I smile to myself, remembering her enthusiasm when they sat us in the Leonard Bernstein section. She's adorable.

"When are you seeing her again?" Grace subtly slides in the question, believing she'll trip me up and catch me lying.

But I won't deny Anni. No matter how it appears, and I know it looks terrible, I won't pretend she doesn't mean the world to me. Even without the extra element of sex that I so desperately crave every fucking goddamn night and day, she makes me happy, merely being in her company.

"She settled into her dormitory this weekend, and I promised her I'd stop by tonight after work to check out her decorating skills. I'm bringing pizza." I wag my eyebrows, convinced Grace will assume pizza is a euphemism for something nasty. I wish it was.

"Pizza, huh?" She smirks and gives me the side-eye.

"Pepperoni," I assure her, then open my office door. Our afternoon meeting lasted longer than expected, and we've got a lot of work to do if I want to leave in time to spend a few hours with Annika.

"Well, well, well... look at what the cat dragged in." Phillip's voice surprises me, and the sound instantly repels me. Grace and I gasp in unison, shocked by the sight of my younger brother sitting at my desk, sporting a shit-eating grin. He's reclined like a king, arms raised and cradling his head with his dirty boots propped on an antique desk that's been in my family for fifty-plus years.

"Yes, just look at what the cat dragged in," I reply sarcastically. "Then vomited all over the carpet. Who the hell let you in here?"

"It was unlocked." He lies. Phillip always lies.

I shake my head and wave my arm, demanding he get out of my chair. "Did you pick the lock?" Of course, he did. The man is a notorious thief and probably rummaged through my drawers while I was out.

"I didn't want to disturb your secretary by hanging

around outside. Sue me for being a considerate person." Every word out of his mouth annoys me to no end.

"How about I sue you for stealing mom's Ming vase and selling it for a fraction of the value. You're lucky I don't call the cops right now," I grumble and shoo him away like a gnat. "I have work to do, Phil. I don't have time for a family reunion."

There was a time when I would have dropped everything to spend time with my little brother. I promised my mother on her deathbed that I wouldn't let our differences tear us apart. Family is family. But enough is enough. I'd need the patience of a saint to keep forgiving his repeated transgressions. He's not a child. He's thirty-eight years old and has yet to work a day in his life.

"I'll come back in twenty minutes. I've got phone calls to make." Grace bolts before Phillip has a chance to pick her pockets.

I wish I could follow, but I'm not about to leave this jackass in my office alone. God only knows how much he's already stolen.

After she leaves, Phil closes the door behind her and takes a seat, lifting one ankle over his knee. I roll my eyes and prepare for his typical speeches. He's out of money but will get out of my hair if I pay him to return to Europe.

"Listen, brother. I'm not here for the usual stuff. I'd like to invite you to dinner and see how you're doing—just the two of us. A lot is going on in my life, and I'd love to tell you all about it." He brushes a hand through his dirty-blond hair, highlighted to make him appear younger, and sighs, pretending to be choked up with emotion.

His dishonesty makes my blood boil with anger. I grit my teeth and clench my fists beneath my desk. Nothing ever surprises me when it comes to Phillip. This is precisely what I'd expect from him.

I hold my palm out and practically beg him to stop talking. "I have a previous engagement."

"Okay, tomorrow." He clasps his hands, rubbing them together like he's warming up for something big.

My rage intensifies every second he lingers.

I swallow the acid clogging my throat and groan. "Just cut your bullshit, Phillip. I'm not interested in hanging out, for old-time's sake. You skipped our mother's funeral but conveniently appeared when it was time to read the will. You blew your inheritance in two years and now randomly appear with your hand out. When I refused to fund your lavish lifestyle, you stole from me, and when I begged you to return it, you blocked me. Our parents left us an equal amount of money. I don't owe you a goddamn thing."

The smile on his smug face vanishes. He's not used to anyone turning him down. Philip still believes he's a charming teenage boy who can talk the panties off the prettiest cheerleader by promising his undying devotion. Well, last time I checked, I don't wear panties.

"You don't have to be a dick. I never mentioned anything about money. I asked you to dinner to tell you about my fiancée. We're marrying next month. The least you can do is congratulate me." He feigns offense and unloads another helping of bullshit.

"Congratulations. Now leave." I switch on my monitor and find the front tab open to my bank's website. Mother fucker was trying to hack into my account. The irritation I've felt since I walked into the room transforms to rage. I turn to face my brother, unable to disguise the festering hatred coursing through my veins. "Get out, asshole."

He jumps to his feet, but he's too dumb to quit while he's ahead. "You don't need so much money, you greedy bastard. You're too big of a prick to marry. Who else do you plan to leave it to?"

I tap the button under my desk, alerting security to remove the intruder in my office. "The only thing you'll inherit from me is a crispy dollar bill to disable any attempts to contest my will. I would rather leave everything to charity than allow you to benefit from my death. And just in case you get any ideas, the new will is already notarized. Don't ever bother me again."

"This isn't over, asshole. I won't let you ruin my life." Phillip flips me off, kicks over a chair, and storms toward the door, just in time to meet the burly security guards tasked with removing him from the building.

Good-fucking-riddance.

CHAPTER 8
ANNI

"Pizza delivery!" I hear a shout at the door and scramble to finish dressing. It's Oliver. Of course, it's Oliver. He said he'd come at 6:00, and it's precisely 5:59. I had a feeling he'd arrive on time.

"Give me a minute!" I yell from across the room, dipping down to pull on my socks, then brushing my damp hair on my way to the door.

Orientation ran late, and the girls from across the hall invited me to join them for a cup of coffee at the student union. I don't drink coffee, but I thought making friends was a good idea. While they jabbered on about classes and boys, I sipped a hot chocolate and tried not to reveal too many details about my life. I'm not embarrassed about growing up in the system. I earned my stripes and have the battle scars to prove it. But most people don't understand, and their first inclination is to pity you. I don't want to be pitied. My life is changing for the better, and so much of it has to do with the man bringing me a medium pepperoni-lover's pizza with extra cheese.

I swing open the door and nearly crash into Oliver's chest.

I skitter onto the balls of my feet, stopping short of knocking him over. His grumpy expression transforms into a smile, and he catches my waist, righting my clumsy legs by pulling me into his embrace. "You're a sight for sore eyes. I've been looking forward to seeing you all day."

"Me?" I catch the doorframe, curling my fingers around the jamb to regain my balance. There's so much I want to say to him. In a little more than a week, he's become more than my benefactor. He's turned into my closest friend. That sounds as ridiculous as it feels, but there's no other way to describe him. A part of me wants to believe he's only being friendly. Why would a man like him want a girl like me? He can have anyone he wants. Women his age would line the streets and perform feats of strength—or something much more intimate—to earn the privilege of being his girlfriend.

I have nothing to offer him. Nothing but my body—which I'm more than happy to relinquish if he were inclined to make a proposition.

"Stop being so humble. I was counting the minutes. Do you know how long it's been since I've had a good slice of pepperoni pizza?" He struts into my tiny dorm carrying the warm box of pizza in the palm of his hand, like a waiter at a pizzeria.

"Extra cheese?" I smile and remind him of my instructions.

"Of course. I wrote everything down—thin crust with extra pepperoni and cheese." He taps his chest, pointing to the notepad he keeps in his coat pocket.

"You're too good to me. I don't think I can ever repay your kindness," I gush, my face reaching boiling point as I try to convey my gratitude without sounding as needy as I feel. If he only knew how much I want to repay him—all the different ways I'm dying to repay him.

Oh God, does that make me a prostitute? Truth be told, I'd do it all for free.

I take the pizza from his hand and place it on my desk, opening the box to enjoy that heavenly aroma. My stomach growls, and I pretend to laugh, hoping to disguise the sound before he hears it.

"It's a good thing I left my afternoon meeting early. It looks like I got here just in time," he teases, winding his sinewy forearm, visible past his rolled-up sleeves, around my waist, and pulling me to him.

I fall against his chest, on top of the world and without a care, when something stiff grazes my back. I flinch but brush it off like I didn't feel a thing. He doesn't move or speak. Neither do I.

There's no way to verify what I felt without peeking over my shoulder and taking a cursory glance at his pants. And that would only make this awkward situation worse. Perhaps, it's best to leave well enough alone.

Maybe I shouldn't have worn such tiny shorts. Was it an act of deliberate entrapment? I don't know. My rational mind is competing with my heart, and they're both in a tug of war with my blossoming libido.

It's not a fair fight.

"I don't have a proper place to eat, but you can take the chair, and I'll sit on the bed. Or we can sit on the rug together. It hasn't had time to get dirty. Whichever you prefer."

He takes two paper plates and two napkins from my stash above the microwave and serves us, gesturing for me to get comfortable on the new shag rug in front of my bed. This is the first time I've allowed him to inspect my new living space. It's a single room with a twin bed, a tiny window, and, fortunately for me, a private bathroom. No matter how much I protested the extra expense, he insisted on that, and I'm eternally grateful.

It might not be much, but it's the first place I've ever had all to myself. And thanks to the graduation gifts I received from Oliver's interns—a handful of gift cards to a local Target

—I could add a few comforts and personal touches. They really didn't have to be so generous, but I have a feeling Oliver bullied them into it.

"Thanks for coming to see me. I know you're a busy man." We sit side by side on the rug with our backs against the frame of my small bed. He's so big he makes it look like something that belongs in Barbie's dream house. His long legs, crossed at the ankle, extend halfway across the room. His big back, tall enough to peek over the top of the mattress, is so broad I need to scoot to one side to give his arms room to move around. Everything about him feels larger than life, but his stature fits his personality. I always feel safe when he's near.

"Thanks for inviting me. I missed you over the weekend, but I know you wanted a chance to settle into your new digs. This is a new adventure for you, and the last thing I want to do is interfere with some coming-of-age rite of passage." His soft chuckle holds an air of insincerity, but he quickly covers his tracks, stuffing his mouth.

"I missed you, too. Saturday was a busy day, setting things up and getting acquainted with some of my neighbors, but I had most of Sunday to myself," I mumble through bites, then dab my mouth with a napkin before I finish my thought. "I binged a new series on Netflix and puttered around campus. It was a pretty uneventful rite of passage.

He groans with displeasure, chewing as he responds, "Why didn't you call me? I would have kept you company. I was so bored, I worked out twice." He flexes his biceps to show me the evidence, as if it isn't crystal clear through the thin fabric of his dress shirt. "Next time, call me. I don't want to hound you to spend time with me, so just assume I'm at your beck and call."

I giggle and lean to one side, digging my shoulder into his arm, which remains steady and unmoving, a testament to my pathetic strength. "I'm at your disposal, Mr. Warbrick. If you want me, all you need to do is say it, text, or call. I'm always ready for you." I don't think about what I say or how it appears. It's not meant to be salacious or a thinly veiled come-on disguised as humor. But that's how he takes it.

Oliver remains silent, staring into space while he gathers his thoughts. He places the remaining slice of his third helping onto the paper plate and puts it to one side. He wipes his hands, straightening his posture before angling his body to face me. His jovial expression suddenly turns serious. "I do want you, Anni. Can't you see I'm desperate for you?"

I've read the mind does funny things to your perception of time, and it's true. How do people react when they get everything they've ever wanted? I've adored this man from a distance for seven years. Meeting him was a thrill. Befriending him felt too good to be true, but hearing him say he wants me? That's the culmination of my fondest dream come true. How can this be real? Why me? Those words repeat in my mind, over and over, growing louder as I try to piece together what I did to deserve this.

"Why me?" I whisper the words under my breath, not realizing I've said them out loud.

He stares, confused, a look of incredulity transforming his dazed expression. His green eyes study me, shifting up and down, side to side, drinking me in without reservation, dropping all pretense concerning his intentions.

He cups my face, lifting my chin until my head falls back on its own. "Don't you know what you do to me, little girl?" Oliver angles his head and leans forward until his lips brush against my throat. He licks my pulse point gently, languidly, lapping at my skin until a warm shiver teases my pulsating core.

I can't think. I can't breathe. His masculine scent envelops me like a blanket, smothering me until I gasp for air. A shuddering moan escapes my parted lips, and I cry out again, unable to contain the hammering beat of my racing heart. "Daddy!"

Oh no.

CHAPTER 9
OLIVER

This is my chance. I don't think she misspoke. She looks horrified, but it wasn't a mistake.

This is what she wants.

This is what we both want.

"Look into my eyes, Anni. Look into my eyes and tell me what you need. Does my little girl need a daddy?" Words I never thought I'd speak emerge with ease. It's the role I was born to play—for her. Only for her. This is what I was always meant to be.

Annika's eyes grow dark, her pupils wide and fathomless. A moment of silence passes between us, and the air around us thickens, gravity weighing us down with unspoken words. Whatever happens next will change the nature of our relationship forever.

I know what I want. And I think I understand what she desires, but until she speaks the words, there is nowhere for us to go.

"I've never had a daddy. What do daddies do?" With her head bowed, she peeks through her lashes and gives me a bashful smile.

I close my eyes and lean forward, pressing my forehead

against hers. The heat of her body radiates into mine and my pulse jumps into the stratosphere. My control slips away, evaporating before my eyes. I've never felt like this before. No one has ever stolen my heart, kicked open the floodgates, and reshaped my world.

"A good daddy takes care of his baby girl in all kinds of ways. He protects her from harm. He satisfies her needs and worships her body with his hands, mouth, and cock. He takes care of her and gives her whatever her little heart desires. But she needs to be a good girl. Are you ready to be Daddy's little girl?" Urgent with need, I curl my hands around her biceps and pull her to me, molding her sweet curves into my hungry embrace. I use one finger to lift her chin and angle my head until our lips are less than an inch apart.

She releases a shuddering breath and places her palms against my chest, curling her fingers into the cotton fabric of my shirt. "Is this wrong? Am I wrong to want this? Why does it feel so right?"

I watch her body stiffen with uncertainty, her tiny hands twisting together as she overcomes whatever shame she feels in asking for what she wants.

"You're young, sweetheart, but old enough to decide for yourself. Do you think it's wrong?" I hold my breath and close the short distance between us. My overwhelming need to taste her sweet swollen lips finally breaks. I lift my hands to her face, cup her jaw, and slam my mouth into hers.

She gasps with surprise, and my tongue darts forward, thrusting, licking, ravishing her innocent lips in a lust-fueled frenzy. I can tell it's her first kiss. She's unsure what to do or how to return my advances, but she tries. Annika struggles to keep my pace, but what she lacks in skill, she makes up with desire. She's perfection—untrained, sinless perfection that I want to thoroughly corrupt and keep for myself.

She's mine. *Mine. Mine Mine.*

"Daddy," she moans through kisses, out of breath but still eager for more.

My body tightens with restraint. I want to kiss her until her lips are bruised. I want to touch her breasts, suck on those tight little nipples, then tongue fuck her pussy until she begs her daddy to make her come. There's no time like the present to make her mine, but I need to let her lead. I haven't been with a virgin since I was seventeen and haven't had sex in years. The molten lava coursing through my veins won't allow me to be gentle, and this beautiful girl needs a tender touch.

At least this one time.

"I've waited so long for you. I think I wished this into life." A soft whisper escapes her lips as she circles her trembling arms around my neck, pressing her full breasts against my heaving chest.

I tighten my grip on her narrow waist and pull her into my lap. She doesn't pull away but settles her hot pussy against my stiff, swollen cock. My eyes roll back in my head when she grinds down, rubbing that sweet cunt against my shaft, driving me crazy when she whispers the words I've longed to hear.

"I'll be whatever you want me to be. Make me your girl good, Daddy."

With those words, the last shreds of my flailing willpower abandon me. Possession and passion consume my every sense and alter my DNA. I feel like the Incredible Hulk, transforming into a wild animal, half man, half beast, whose mission in life has forever changed.

Annika needs a daddy. And this daddy needs his little girl.

"Do you really want me to make you mine, angel? Daddy has a big cock." I place her hand over the bulge in my jeans and make her touch me. My rigid shaft jerks against the apex of her thighs, spilling precum inside my boxers. This beautiful girl makes me feel like a teenager. Every emotion feels brand new. "When I slide this inside you, I might split that tiny pussy in two... not once, not twice, but every fucking day for the rest of your life, little girl. Once your daddy gets a taste of what belongs to him, he won't be able to be without it."

She slides her bottom lip between her teeth and nods. "I don't care if it hurts. I need you. Your little girl needs her daddy now."

My wicked thoughts darken to an inky black abyss, but I force a smile to keep her from reading my mind and running out the door. "You are already mine, baby. And Daddy is going to make sure you never forget it."

Annika is my new purpose. My soulmate and reason for living. I've always been a man who went after what he wanted. I've chased every dream and worked fucking hard to turn them into reality. Annika's different. I should have stated my intentions from the start because she isn't a deal that needs to be settled or a company that has to be conquered.

I'm taking what I want now. No more waiting and wishing. We found each other for a reason. This is far beyond the lusty needs of a sick man infatuated with a teenage girl. This is kismet. I was born to love this little girl, and that's precisely what I'll do.

Starting now.

CHAPTER 10
OLIVER

"I've thought about this for a long time." She pulls away from my embrace, but her dreamy gaze remains locked on mine as she tugs the butter-soft t-shirt over her head.

My jaw ticks, and my muscles tense with anticipation. There are so many things I need to say and so many things I want to do. Every moment that passes feels like an eternity of torture.

"How long… sweetheart?" I gulp and swallow the lump in my throat, watching her push the bra straps off her shoulders. Because I'm a greedy bastard who can't wait his turn, I unfasten the front latch, nothing but a tiny flower keeping the breasts of my dreams from spilling out into my palms. The indescribable sight makes me gasp, my breath catching in my throat. Perfect mounds of supple flesh fall into my hands, and my heart skips a beat, a gentle reminder that I need to stifle my urges before I lose total control.

She's never been touched. Never had a man ravish her innocent body with the feral need of a wild animal intent on mating. She's the most precious thing in my life, and I don't want to scare her away by giving in to every sick desire all at once. There will be time for that later. We have the rest of our lives to experience every fiendish fantasy currently swirling through my lust-addled brain.

"I've wanted this for years, Daddy. When I was eleven, I saw a photo of you in the newspaper and dreamed you were my long-lost father. You were so handsome and powerful, and I was so alone and scared. I fantasized you'd show up one day to save me." Her words break my heart and temporarily halt my busy hands.

"Sweetheart, if I'd known, I would have searched high and low to find you." My words come out in a rush fueled by pure emotion. This beautiful girl was lonely in this great big city, needing my help, wanting me to rescue her from her terrible situation. I was alone in my ivory tower, inexplicably missing a piece of my soul.

"That's not the way it was supposed to be. I knew that then and I know it now." She lifts my hands and places them on her breasts. I instinctively mold them into my palms, kneading her flesh and waiting with bated breath for her to continue.

"Then those feelings turned into something else. I learned what men and women do in the dark and how they love each other and make each other feel good. And whenever I imagined doing those things, you're the only man that came to mind. This is what I want, Daddy. This is what I've waited for. Please... make me yours." At this moment, Annika Bennett effectively blows my mind, tattoos my heart with her name, and makes me her slave.

It takes me a moment to regain my composure. I've never been in love and never imagined an eighteen-year-old girl would walk into my office, sweep me off my feet and bring me to my knees. My cock throbs, thickening to impossible proportions in my pleated slacks. It will take a hell of a lot more pleats to hide the fire-breathing dragon ready to tear through the wool and wreak havoc on her unsuspecting pussy.

"Come here, baby girl. Daddy needs you to take away the pain." I curl my hand around her neck, thread my fingers through her long auburn hair, and run my tongue across her soft bottom lip. She tastes so fucking sweet. So ripe. So mine. This indulgence will have lasting consequences for both of us, but there's no going back to what we were before.

"I'll be a good girl for my daddy. Tell me where it hurts, and I'll make it better," she purrs like a kitten and draws my tongue into her mouth. I seal my lips to hers, devouring her soft whispers until my rabid need takes control. I plunge my tongue into her mouth, exploring every recess, tasting every kiss and asking for more, punishing her pouty lips for making me so weak. She has me wrapped around her pinky, a glutton for her love, a slave to her whims. From this day forward, I'm an empty husk without her and a god when she's by my side.

"Daddy's going to make you feel good first, baby girl. You will always come first." I mold my hands to her round ass, lift her into my arms and carry her onto the bed. She lands softly on the mattress, eyes closed and breasts bouncing. I gnash my teeth impatiently as I slide her thin shorts, with barely enough material to cover her ass, off her smooth legs. My gaze is immediately drawn to the moist patch of cotton between her thighs. My eyes widen with avarice. She's so wet, the fabric clings to her skin, conformed to the naughty cleft like a second skin.

"How did I wind up with such a bad girl?" I slip my fingers beneath the string at her hip and pull her panties down, my eyes fixed on the thick arousal that smears across her skin.

She arches her back and spreads her legs, brazenly offering her innocent pussy—so pink, swollen with nothing to hide it but a tiny thatch of auburn curls. Her eyes hood and burn into mine, tempting me to do what I came here to do. Make her mine. Claim her virginal body and take her home forever. As much as I appreciate her enthusiasm for this place, it will never be good enough for my girl. I will never be able to live my life every day and night without having her close.

I crawl onto the bed and wedge my shoulder between her soaked thighs. The scent of her arousal knocks me senseless. I blink away the daze and focus on Annika's pussy, so primed and ready for me, my eyes practically brim with tears. It's the hottest thing I've ever seen and an image I'll never forget. But it's not nearly enough. I want more. I want to know what she sounds like when she comes and looks like when I drive every inch into her virgin pussy.

"Daddy, please don't keep me waiting," she whispers, moaning under her breath as her hands caress her breasts, tweaking her nipples for my viewing pleasure. I could faint, but there's no time for that. There's too much to do before I rest.

"Don't rush me, little girl. Daddy doesn't like a brat."

She clamps her mouth shut, her eyes wide with curiosity and lust.

I run two fingers down her slit and gather moisture before bringing them to my mouth. The taste awakens the savage beast who's had his first taste of the forbidden. I'll never be the same, and that's fucking fine with me. "There's no going back, baby girl. Now that Daddy's found you and knows how sweet you taste, he'll never let you out of his sight."

Enough bullshit. Enough buildup. The bed is so small there's no way to lie between her legs and service her the way she needs. Frustrated with my growing need and motivated by my desire to bury my mouth between her legs, I clasp her ankle, slide my hand beneath her ass and lift her pussy straight onto my tongue.

"Daddy!" Her head falls back, and her voice jumps an octave. My tongue slides along the seam of her sex, frantic, wild, licking and spearing her parted, sodden lips. She claws the blanket, searching for purchase as her hips convulse, slamming her pussy into my hungry mouth.

I'm ravenous for my girl, crazed with lust and weak with love for a woman I need to own. I don't want anyone else touching her, looking at her, believing for one second that I'd ever let them take her away from me. Before the night is through, she'll know in no uncertain terms that her body and heart belong to her daddy.

"You're mine, angel. Do you understand that?" I tease her with my tongue, lashing her clit in tiny circles until her muscles tighten and her toes curl.

She yelps, nodding frantically as I suckle that tiny bundle of nerves and devour all the sticky arousal that flows freely from her quivering pussy, nearly choking on the taste of her climax. It's so thick it coats my beard, and I smear it in, hoping it takes days to wash it out.

"I'm yours." Her breath hitches as tiny squeals escape her parted lips, climbing in frequency as she reaches the pinnacle and flies over the cliff. She twists, thrashing as wave after wave crash over her, holds her underwater, and drowns her in bliss.

I fall forward and slant my mouth over hers, stealing her breath and melting in her warmth. Our tongues dance, licking, swiping, losing ourselves in kiss after kiss until I pull away and stare into her eyes, thoroughly in love. "I want all of you, Anni. Every part. Every piece. I'll never share you or give you up. Daddy would be so lost without his little girl."

She nods, and her eyes glaze with need. My mouth falls to the curve of her neck, and I drop my hands to her breasts, squeezing, kneading, then dipping my mouth to take a stiff nipple between my teeth. She purrs, whimpering as I nibble on sensitive flesh, pulling and suckling until my escalating desire demands I make her mine.

"Are you ready for me?" I step off the bed and remove my shirt and pants so quickly it defies the laws of physics.

Buttons pop, pants rip, and I'm pretty sure my watch breaks when I toss it across the room. It doesn't matter. I'll buy another, but I'll never return to this time and place again. Pleasing Anni is the only thing that matters. I need to fuck her, consume her, and make her so addicted to my cock, she never stops coming back for more. With a twenty-two-year age gap, I never want her to doubt my virility.

"So ready, Daddy." She nods slowly, and for a moment, I take her in, the look of love in her eyes, the sheen of sweat covering her dewy skin, and the sensuality vibrating off her limbs. She's the most gorgeous thing I've ever seen and the epitome of sex.

I'm the luckiest son of a bitch alive.

"I need you..." she whispers, her eyes focused on my stiff cock jutting forward, poised between her legs, inches from her core. She's wet and primed for me. She may even be ripe. There are no condoms in sight, and I have no intention of ever wearing one with her.

Whatever happens, happens.

I spread her legs and trail the head of my cock down the seam of her sex. She jerks forward, bucking her hips when the crown bumps against her swollen clit. "I'm sorry if this hurts, baby girl. This tiny pussy needs to make room for Daddy's cock, and it may take a couple of tries." Every word that spills from my lips makes me harder than steel. I don't care if anyone thinks it's wrong or taboo. Nothing has ever felt more right than this.

"Don't hold back. I've waited so long for you to make a real woman, Daddy." Her words make me sway. There's so much blood in my cock, I fear it's siphoned too much from my brain.

"Sweet baby girl." I ease into her, parting her folds with the head of my cock, and watch her face twist with pain. "Look at me, sweetheart. Lower your head and watch Daddy's big cock make a woman out of you."

Anni's eyes grow wide as I slide inside her, stretching her tight walls inch by inch until I wedge myself halfway in. She exhales and lifts her hips, looking for more, wanting the rest. "More. I can take more." Beads of sweat dot her forehead and roll down her face. "Don't make me wait anymore. Let me take the pain away, Daddy."

I stiffen, remembering my filthy words, and smile. "You're such an eager girl, but you look so sweet, I don't think I can say no." I lean forward, cover her body, and plunge all the way in. Her nails dig into my biceps, holding me steady until her tight walls adjust to my brutal invasion. I pull out slowly, rutting gently, working my way back in until there's nowhere else to go. I repeat the motion, building friction, watching her tense expression soften as her inner muscles learn to accept me.

"It's okay, baby. Daddy's going to make it feel better. He loves his good girl. And he loves this little pussy so much he'll have it for breakfast, lunch, and dinner, every fucking day." I lick her bottom lip and lower my mouth to hers, kissing her fiercely, distracting her from my thrusting cock until I know the pain has finally transformed into a pleasurable ache in search of release. She wraps her calves around my hips, grinding, rolling her hips as she takes every inch of my pulsing, driving cock and whimpers for more, harder, and faster strokes. I clasp my hands in hers, amazed by her libido and astounded by how hard I've fallen for my little girl.

"Oh, Daddy! Daddy! I'm so close." Her back bows. Her hips buck, and her pussy clenches, milking my cock as she climbs the heights of her second orgasm. I hold on to her narrow waist, thrusting with even strokes, pummeling her untrained pussy like a battering ram until my balls tighten and a rush of euphoria makes me fall into her arms.

"Fuck. Fuck. Fuck." I clasp her hands, and hold them over our heads. My cock jerks. My muscles tense. I erupt like a bull, groaning, gasping, and painting her walls with jets of hot, sticky cum. There's so much it spills between us and soaks her thighs. I hold her for a moment, kissing, whispering words of love and promises that this is only the beginning.

And I mean every word.

It's only the beginning.

CHAPTER 11
ANNI

"You're avoiding the inevitable, my love. Enough dragging your feet. I want you moved in by the end of the day." Oliver fumbles with the hem of my skirt and scolds me while his busy hand slides into the seam of my panties. I lean into his broad chest and angle my hips, lifting my thigh off the bench seat of his custom Rolls Royce. He's incorrigible, and I'm his satisfied enabler.

"You spent so much money on my dorm room, and I thought maybe I'd keep it just in case... you know," I whimper as I try to make my point, unable to finish my thought as his fingers slide through my slick folds and make contact with my clit. I dig my forehead into his chest and listen to the beat of my racing heart while grinding shamelessly against his stroking hand.

"Just in case?" He teases my clit, batting it with his thumb while dipping his fingers into my pussy. Oliver does everything on instinct. He doesn't need to look at what he's doing to me.

I plead my case, lost in the delicious strokes of his talented fingers, and he simply stares ahead at the road, peeved with my lack of cooperation.

"You know... what I mean." The words come out in a shuddering cry as I hang onto his lapels and try to stifle the sound of my moans. The privacy screen isn't in place, and I'm almost sure his driver can hear me. I reach for the button, but Oliver blocks my access with his arm.

"Are you having second thoughts, little girl?" He picks up the pace, stroking his thumb to the rhythm of his thrusting fingers.

My hips move on their own. My breath labors. I'm close— *so close.*

"Never, Daddy..." I whine, my head dipping so low I feel the warmth from his towering erection inches from my face. I move my head back and forth, and let my open mouth graze the top of his cock, tempting him to release the monster lurking within. Last night was the first time he'd let me take him in my mouth, and I'm anxious to try it again.

Maybe this time, he'll let me take him until the end.

Oliver curls his fist in my hair and lifts my head so we're eye to eye. His fingers move faster, rougher, polishing my clit, plunging in and out, in and out, rubbing the soft place inside me with such precision I come without further delay. It hits me like a bolt of lightning, shocking my system with currents of electricity that leave me a babbling, drooling mess.

This is the way he bends me to his will.

"Fine! You can move my things!" I'm such a sap. But in my defense, he's amazing.

He licks his fingers salaciously and smiles. "Keep your dorm room, sweetheart. But I want you with me. I hurt my back sleeping in that twin bed, trying to satisfy your insatiable needs."

The car slows and drifts toward the curb in front of Oliver's building. I narrow my gaze and raise my chin with defiance, making sure I hop out of his car with a bounce that lifts my skirt high enough to show half my thighs.

Oliver is on me like a light switch. He groans and leads

me into the building with his hand wound tightly around my arm. "That was uncalled for, little girl," he murmurs, smiling at the men and women gathered in the busy lobby as we walk toward his private elevator.

I slide into the elevator and type his special code before he has time to scoot all the way in. He darts inside and gives me a stern expression that promises repercussions. Sometimes I just can't help egging him on. He knows he brings out the brat in me. As soon as the doors close, he pins me to the back of the car and wraps my legs around his waist. It's only been two weeks since we met and one week since we first made love, and I'm already addicted to his kisses... and so much more.

"Why must you test me? Do you want Daddy to punish that little pussy again before dinner? I have a surprise for you, but I don't believe bad girls deserve presents." He nuzzles his face into my neck and exhales.

My body shakes with rabid anticipation, trembling as his cock digs into my wet panties, still fresh from my climax. I'm a glutton for that heat-seeking missile that always knows precisely what target to strike.

"I'm sorry, Daddy. Please forgive me!" I giggle, tensing my thigh muscles to tighten my grip on his waist while kicking my feet excitedly.

"Always, baby girl. Always." Oliver closes his lips over mine in a gentle kiss that sends shivers down my spine.

"Do you love me, baby girl?" He squeezes my ass cheeks, pinching me until I squeal.

I nod with confidence and absolute sincerity. "Always, Daddy. Always."

The doors slide open, and an unfamiliar voice greets our arrival. "Well, isn't this sweet? Looks like fussy old Oliver has got himself a sugar baby."

I gasp, unlock my ankles and let my feet fall to the floor.

Sugar baby? What does that mean? Is that what people call someone like me?

Oliver's smile fades instantly, his jaw ticks, and his face grows an interesting shade of red. His features sharpen, and anger burns in his gaze. I've never seen him angry, and by the looks of it, I'm not sure I ever want to see it again.

"How the hell did you get up here?" Oliver bellows, clutching my hand and leading me down the hall toward his front door. He obviously knows this man, but he fails to share his identity with me. As we approach the door, Oliver digs into his coat pocket, pulls out his phone, and yells obscenities at what I assume is building security.

The man follows us, smug and defiant. "Oh, come on, big brother. I've only come to say goodbye."

Brother? *Oliver has a brother?* He told me his entire family was dead. What else is this man hiding?

"Goodbye, Phillip. Leave now before security hands you over to the cops, and your departure is again delayed. I don't have anything to say to you." Oliver unlocks the door and nudges me inside, his hand trembling as he slips in behind me.

"What's going on?" I hide behind him, frazzled by his brother's appearance and Oliver's rage.

"Nothing, sweetheart. Go upstairs and get ready. We don't want to be late for tonight. I won't let him ruin your surprise." He tries to remain calm, but the anger simmering beneath the surface is too powerful to contain.

"Yes. Hurry up, darling. You don't want my brother to subtract from your fee." Phillip peeks past Oliver and makes a joke at my expense. He attempts to give me a patronizing smirk, but a direct hit from Oliver's clenched fist wipes the smug expression off his face.

I jump back, frightened by the violence and instantly titillated by him defending my honor. *This is a first.*

"Don't look at her. Don't talk to her. And don't you dare

fucking speak to her. I'm not giving you any more money. Not now. Not ever." Oliver slams the door and turns to face me, his expression marred with regret.

"I'm sorry, sweetheart. That's my younger brother, Phillip. He's a thief and an all-around terrible person. I disowned him years ago, but he still comes around whenever he needs money. He thinks if he gives me enough trouble, I'll pay him off to make him disappear from my life. If you ever see him loitering nearby, call me and then call the police. I don't trust him." He releases a sharp breath and walks into my embrace.

"I'm sorry." I rest my head on his chest and try to say something comforting. "If it's any consolation, he looks nothing like you."

"Thank you for that. But I'm the one who's sorry you had to meet him this way. Please don't take anything he said to heart. He was trying to goad me, and no doubt he could tell you're important to me." He leans forward and plants a kiss on my forehead. "Let's forget about this asshole and get dressed. I think you'll like my surprise."

CHAPTER 12
ANNI

Oliver winds his hand around my waist and leads me through the crowded room, gently stroking the small of my back to soothe my escalating nerves. My surprise is a night at the opera and it's so much more than a glamorous night out. He knows what the theater means to me. I told him about my mother's love for opera and he made another wish come true.

"Why are you shaking, sweetheart? Are you cold?" Oliver wraps his powerful arm around me and lovingly brings me into his warmth. I shiver again—not from the chilly temperature, but the delicious scent of his cologne.

"I feel underdressed," I confess under my breath, petrified I'll embarrass him. I'm not accustomed to being the center of attention. We're surrounded by beautiful women decked in diamonds with impeccable pedigrees and refined taste. Their eyes are trained on the wealthiest, most handsome man in the room, but his gaze never leaves me. No one's ever placed me on a pedestal before, and the last thing I want to do is let him down.

"Nonsense. You're the most beautiful woman here. I feel like the luckiest man alive," he whispers, nuzzling my cheek with his as I lean into his towering physique for stability. As uncomfortable as I feel, this might be the happiest I've ever been. I'm on Oliver's arm, by his side, and basking in the glow of his adoration.

Is this what love looks like? When I was younger, love looked like my mother, a woman I only remember from a handful of photographs I kept in an ancient cigar box. I can't recall her voice, the scent of her perfume, or the touch of her hand on my cheek. But until the day I fell for Oliver Warbrick, that was the only love I could fathom.

Is it possible for two people to fall in love so fast? I loved him for years before we met, but that childish infatuation can't compare to how much my feelings have grown since we met. He proclaims to love me and I don't want to doubt him. But is this real?

We've shared so much and said things I'd never be able to repeat to another living soul. The memory of our morning lovemaking is still fresh in my mind. I can't stop thinking about the look in his eyes, the beat of his heart, and the thrusting rhythm of his massive cock.

How can I manage so much? How on earth does he make it fit? And why am I always ready for more?

I want this to be real, but how does someone who's never been loved recognize the real thing?

"I'm the lucky one." I sink into his loving embrace and follow his lead as we ascend a narrow staircase toward our box seats. I'm overcome with excitement. My mother dreamed of singing at Lincoln Center, but no one ever fostered her singing or supported her dreams. She didn't have an Oliver in her life.

But how could she? There's no one quite like... *Daddy.*

My cheeks catch fire, still amazed he wants me to call him that whenever we're alone. It was my deepest, darkest wish to have a daddy like him. Someone to love and care for me the way no one has before. But he's a different kind of daddy, a perfect man who loves me in all the best ways.

"I don't accept your evaluation of our relationship, little girl. I've waited my whole life to meet you. You're a breath of fresh air in my dull world, and made me fall madly in love with you." He leans down and kisses my head, inhaling deeply before pulling away. "As much as I want to see you enjoy this opera, I can't wait to get you alone. I'm already hard thinking about tasting that sweet pussy again." He lewdly licks his fingers, the same ones he used to make me come moments ago.

I cover my mouth, suddenly bashful after shamelessly offering to suck his cock in the car. And fortunately, he doesn't buy it for a minute. Oliver pulls out my chair and helps gather the hem of my dress before kneeling beside me, his hand trailing back and forth against my thigh. "Tell me the truth, baby girl. Is your little pussy still hungry for my cock?"

My eyes shoot out of my skull. Flushed, hot, and bothered, I look over my shoulder to make sure the usher hasn't lingered long enough to hear us, then exhale a sigh of relief when I see he's gone. As much as I want to protest, I can't. Oliver's dirty words never fail to turn my simmering lust into a raging wildfire. So much has changed between us. He came on so strong and fast I could hardly catch my breath. But I wouldn't change a thing. I just never thought I'd fall for a man with such a filthy mouth.

I nod, cup his chin, and run my fingers along his chiseled jaw. "I'm ravenous, Daddy. Absolutely famished."

He exhales a shaky breath and stares at my mouth, licking his lips. "Mark my words, little girl. I'll turn you into a glutton for cock if it's the last thing I do."

"I believe you." My pulse quickens with anticipation of things to come.

Oliver's green eyes hood with desire. He lifts my hand to

his lips and murmurs, "You make it hard to control my need for you. But just this once, I'll try. At least until intermission." He pushes his chair closer to mine and sits, groaning as he adjusts his stiff cock. My thighs clench, and my hunger deepens at the sight of his massive bulge, remembering the wonderful things it makes me feel. The scent of his skin and the fragrant aroma of his delicious cologne makes it hard to think of anything other than sliding beneath him and letting him have his way with me. But for the sake of our romantic and pricey evening, I push my urges aside and concentrate on the stage.

"Thank you for bringing me here tonight," I whisper through tight lips, afraid I'll speak too loud and draw unwanted attention. He wants me to relax and enjoy the experience, and I know I should be used to judgment, but it never gets easier. What if he takes a good look at me once the afterglow fades, under the harsh lights of reality, and decides he's made a horrible mistake?

I lean forward and watch the audience below take their seats. We're the closest box seats to the stage, and although it feels private, we're not hidden from view. The same haughty women who rudely glared when I walked into Lincoln Center hand in hand with Oliver Warbrick gather at the front and file into cramped orchestra seats that undoubtedly cost thousands. They try to be demure, occasionally glancing in our direction and are probably wondering if I'm a hired escort or kept woman.

Is that what everyone thinks I am? Was Phillip right to assume that? Am I Oliver's sugar baby?

"What are you thinking about, sweetheart?" Oliver leans forward and threads his fingers through my hair, brushing the falling tendrils off my face. He caresses my chin, lifting it until our eyes meet in a heated gaze that sends tingles down my spine. His stern expression makes me shiver. "Why do you look unhappy?"

He notices everything. Even when I try to hide my emotions from him, he always sees through my façade.

I duck my head, fearing my insecurity will make him rethink our relationship. He has no idea how much his loss would break me. "This is new to me. I promise I'm trying to learn how to live in your world, but it might take some time."

Oliver cocks his head to one side and narrows his gaze with confusion. I watch the play of emotions on his face and then find reassurance in his eyes. "You don't need to try to fit into anything, sweetheart. You're my world, and I'll fit into you."

"Is that sexual?"

He chuckles and slides closer, wrapping an arm around my shoulder. "Well, now it is."

CHAPTER 13
OLIVER

I stare at my watch, eyeing the little hand and waiting for it to mark off another minute. How long does it take to use the bathroom? I should have gone with her, but she insisted on making me stay to fill her in on whatever she missed. It was a mistake. No one takes fifteen minutes in the middle of the show. I know the ladies' rooms are notoriously crowded, and I'd expect this during intermission, but that's another twenty minutes away.

That's it. I've had enough. I understand she needs privacy. And I'm well aware that my territorial behavior over the past week has grown odious at best, but she can't expect me not to worry when she struts about the city with a dangerous level of naivete. She grew up in the system, and she's demonstrated her street smarts more than once, but she's also under the grave misconception that she's an ordinary girl who can don a pair of jeans and a hoodie and blend into the background.

Annika Bennett will never blend in. Jeans make her ass look incredible; every man's hands hunger to spank it. A hoodie does a piss poor job of hiding the voluptuous breasts

I've come to know and love. Her long red hair makes her look like a fiery Norse goddess granting you the key to heaven.

She thinks I'm a generous man with a benevolent soul who offered to make her dreams come true without strings attached. But I had ulterior motives from the start, dreams that transformed into a reality faster than any man deserves. She came to me a wide-eyed innocent girl looking for a father figure, and I twisted her desires into something dark, dirty, and a thousand times better than I ever imagined. I'm a fallen man with no desire to be saved.

The more I corrupt her, the more I revel in my downfall.

I'm going to marry that girl. I'm going to beg her to be my wife before she comes to her senses and figures out that I'm nothing but a rich, dirty old man with a mind to baby-trap her into loving me forever. Now, where the hell is she?

I slink out of my seat, careful not to make any noise or draw attention away from the stage. If I were seated downstairs, ushers would swarm and force me to remain, but box seats get special privileges. We can come and go as long as we don't make a raucous.

The hallway is empty and there are no signs of Anni. This concerns me. A part of me hoped she was waiting for a good time to reenter the box, nervous she might make too much noise. But there are no signs of her or anyone else.

An usher comes into view at the top of the stairs, and I quietly ask him for directions to the ladies' room. He looks confused but points me towards the left, down a slender aisle overlooking the lobby downstairs. I rush forward, carrying Annika's wrap and evening bag, looking like a clueless husband in search of his wife. The more I hear those words, the more they suit me.

And I hope they'll work for her too.

I step close to the door marked Ladies and lift my hand, tapping lightly and whispering her name. "Anni. Are you in there, baby?"

A woman steps out and raises her fists in a protective stance. Although she appears frightened by my looming presence, I take the chance to inquire about my girl. "Forgive me, but was there another woman inside. I'm looking for my girlfriend. She disappeared twenty minutes ago and hasn't returned to our seats."

Her expression softens with concern. "I'm sorry. I was the only person inside. And no one came in since I arrived." She doesn't appear to be lying, but that doesn't mean I trust her with something so important. When she turns the corner, I barge through the door, check under every stall, then kick open every door. She's nowhere in sight.

Annika's gone.

CHAPTER 14
ANNI

"I don't understand. Where are you taking me?" I mumble through my poorly placed gag, with my hands tied behind my back, and roll around on the leather upholstery of Phillip's car. I don't think he understands me; if he does, he's chosen not to answer. His clothes are disheveled, and his hair looks unwashed. His backseat is littered with trash and stinks like body odor and stale cigarettes. He's the complete opposite of Oliver.

I should have been more careful. Daddy wanted to follow me out, watch me, and care for me in case I got lost, but I stood firm and asked to go alone. He worries so much, and I accused him of being overprotective. How could I have predicted this?

Phillip appeared out of the blue, standing silently in a darkened hall a few feet from the ladies' room. My mind was on other things, and I let my guard down in front of the fancy people. Since I met Oliver, I've walked around with my head in the clouds and forgotten his world can sometimes be just as dangerous as mine. The only thing on my mind was returning to my seat and confessing my insecurities to the man I love. He's been so good to me. He deserves to know the truth, even if it exposes my deepest vulner-ability.

I spent most of my life as an unwanted orphan. It isn't easy to adjust from eighteen years of abandonment and indifference to Oliver's over-the-top attention and adoration. It's lovely but a little terrifying.

It took me a second to determine that it was Phillip in disguise. I hadn't heard his voice long enough to recognize the sound, and the dark wig covering his fair hair threw me off. Before I realized what was happening, he covered my mouth with his giant hand—a trait he shares with Oliver—and dragged me into an empty stairwell. Hauling me downstairs, carrying me like a sack of potatoes, he muttered obscenities about Oliver's money, the will, and my inconvenient presence in his life. None of it made sense. Oliver and I have known one another for two weeks.

How could Phillip perceive me as a threat?

I can be brave. Oliver will come for me. He promised to always take care of me, and I believe him. Growing up in the foster system, orphans like me live in survival mode. I always managed to stay on the right side of the law, but I knew many kids who couldn't. They weren't bad, but life taught them to be cunning, doing whatever they could to survive. Not everyone is as fortunate as me. Oliver is the first person I've ever trusted with my life, and I know he won't disappoint. Good girls trust their daddies.

Phillip doesn't seem to know what he's doing. He wants money. He's a spoiled man who's been given everything in life and doesn't know how to survive on his own. Oliver shared a few details about their relationship on the way to Lincoln Center. Phillip's desperation has caused him to take drastic measures to achieve his goals.

Perhaps he wants to ransom me.

What precisely am I worth?

Panic and curiosity rack my brain. He said he wouldn't

harm me, but unstable people make mistakes. I know Oliver will come. When he finally discovers I'm missing, I know he'll search for me. He said he loves me, and although I have no experience being on the receiving end of this emotion, I'm inclined to believe someone who shows it as much as he does probably isn't lying.

I shouldn't doubt him. Daddy won't let me down.

While Phillip weaves in and out of traffic at an unsustainable speed bound to draw attention from New York's finest, I fumble with my hands, wiggling them hard enough to give me slack. I should have tried this earlier, but I needed a few minutes to assess the situation before I made my move. When I've freed my hands, I remove my gag, flip over, and take a long look at my surroundings. We're less than two blocks from Oliver's place. Why would he take me there?

"What are you going to do to me?" I ask, rubbing my face and wiping the saliva off my chin.

Phillip swerves and screams like a girl when a massive truck nearly sideswipes us into the curb. "How the hell did you get loose?" He glares at me through the rearview mirror, stunned by my Houdini-like ways.

I contemplate escaping at the light, but fear keeps me glued to the seat. I didn't see a weapon, but I'm not taking any chances.

"Oliver will come. It's not too late to stop this." I make veiled threats, hoping to frighten him with his brother's wrath while searching the street for signs of Daddy. He must have figured out something's wrong by now.

"I'm not going to hurt you, Annika. That's your name, right? I just need your help." He double parks and points to Oliver's building, his eyes gleaming with ideas he's too nervous to properly articulate. "We don't have much time. You have a key. And the doorman knows you." He runs a shaky hand through his tousled hair and pulls at the roots with frustration.

I stare, confused, unsure what he means and wondering if this is a bad time to tell him I left my bag with his brother. He exits the car, speed walking while he glances over his shoulder, looking more suspicious than a bank robber.

The far-off sound of sirens makes him flinch. He freezes, looking left to right as he opens my door and yanks my arm, wrenching me out with such force I fall forward onto the street. I land on my hands, catching myself before my face makes contact with hot asphalt. He groans, furious I'm holding him up and visually panicked by the high-pitched screech of skidding cars.

"You son of a bitch!"

I'd know that voice anywhere. Oliver jumps out of a moving car, fists first, with a look of terror. He's here. I knew he'd come. I knew Daddy would save me.

"Anni!" He sprints to my side, his echoing footfalls vibrating against the street as I struggle to crawl to my feet, desperate to feel him in my arms.

Police cars surround us, and four men wearing Kevlar under black suits swarm like wasps, taking Phillip to the ground. I rush out of their way, shocked by their roughness and mesmerized by the blue and red lights converging from all sides. Oliver saved me, and he brought the cavalry with him.

"Baby girl, are you okay? Did he hurt you?"

My heart swells with love. A broken heel makes me stumble into a nearby car, but Oliver swoops in just in time to catch me. He doesn't hold back, and neither do I. So many things could have gone wrong. I'm lucky. We're lucky.

"Little girl, you just gave me the scare of a lifetime," he groans into my skin and peppers my face with kisses.

My body shakes as the adrenaline coursing through my veins begins to wear off, and I struggle to speak, words tripping over my quivering lips. I shake my head and rest it on his chest, comforted by the warmth of his soothing arms. "I'm okay. He scared me, but he didn't hurt me."

"Are you sure? Tell Daddy what he did to you. I'll send that bastard straight to hell if he hurt a single hair on your head." His angry tone sends a rush of heat to my core. Looking for sympathy and Daddy's special care, I purposely rub my wrists, still raw from my restraints, and offer them to him, expecting sweet kisses to make them better.

He quickly complies, massaging each one before bringing them to his lips. "Where the fuck is he? That piece of shit isn't getting away with this. We're pressing charges. He could have hurt you. He could have killed you, which means I would have killed him. Not only did he put you in danger, but that motherfucker almost turned me into a murderer." He scans the crowd of police, looking for signs of his brother, grinding his teeth and breathing fire.

I tear him away and lead him into the building before he does something he'll regret. The police have it covered, and I need time alone to recover. Special time. Daddy time. "Maybe you should give him enough money to get out of town and be done with him?"

"Absolutely not!" he growls, then lowers his voice when I shrink. "Sorry, sweetheart. That piece of filth needs to pay, and there's no way in hell I'll reward him for jeopardizing your safety and scaring the shit out of me. For a few moments, I thought you left me." He lowers his gaze and curls me into his embrace, holding me tighter than I've ever been held.

"Never," I assure him. "What kind of little girl leaves her daddy?"

"A bad girl. And you're not a bad girl, are you?"

"Me? Never."

———

"Bad girl. Bad, bad girl. Holy shit, you make me crazy, little girl."

We fall through the front door, lips locked, arms entwined, unable to get enough to satisfy our needs. I feel unhinged and insane. His lips are perfection. His hands have a mind of their own. Everything he does, everywhere he touches, brings me to the edge.

"Daddy, I need you!" I scream with pleasure, lost in a mad haze of lust, tearing my insides apart.

He made me this way. He turned me into a sex-crazed bad girl who needs to worship his thick cock night and day. How did I lose my way? How did he work his magic so fast?

He unbuttons his shirt and tosses his cufflinks on an entryway table. One rolls to the floor, and I bend to retrieve it. Oliver takes this fortuitous opportunity to pounce. I hardly see it coming. "Daddy's here, baby. Daddy's here."

Oliver positions me on my hands and knees and bends forward, pressing his chest against my back.

"Daddy, let's go to bed," I whisper, trembling as his mouth lingers on my neck and his hips piston into mine—dry humping me with his steely erection.

"I can't wait, baby girl. I need this pussy now, and you're not going to deny me, are you?" His deep voice and stern tone make me shiver. He knows I can't say no when he takes control. How could I deny him when he masters my body with such ease and rabid enthusiasm? Ever since the first time he made me come, he perpetually preys on my neediness to get his way.

His hands drift to my thighs, where he gathers my hem and lifts it over my ass, exposing my bare cheeks. He palms each one, growling as he sinks his teeth into my flesh and licks the lacy strap down my crack. "I know you're wet. I don't even have to look, little girl. I can smell it from here." He inhales deeply, and my body warms, tingling with antic-ipation.

"I'm so wet, Daddy." I wiggle my behind, and he catches the tiny string, snapping it between his fingers. My pussy is completely exposed to his view, and I'm so ready for him.

"I really do have a bad girl on my hands." Oliver fists his cock and slides it between my cleft, nudging my clit with every pass.

I whimper, crazy with lust but too afraid to beg for it. I'm a good girl. A good, good girl.

"Daddy, please..." I whisper, urging him on without really saying it.

"Please, what, baby girl? Use your words," he taunts me.

"Please, give it to me," I whine, grinding onto his cock, searching for relief.

"Say it, little girl. Say it, or I'm putting it back in my pants," he threatens with the worst possible scenario, and I cave.

"Give me your cock, Daddy. Please, give it to me now," I beg, sexual frustration oozing from every pore. There's no room for shame anymore. I'm hot, bothered, and need to get off again.

"Tell me you love me, baby girl." Before I can answer, he thrusts forward and buries the entire length of his stiff cock, stealing my breath in the process.

I gasp, too full to respond. He pulls out and eases back in, rocking gently, taking languid strokes to warm me up. But that time has passed.

"I love you, Daddy. Your baby girl loves you." The words come out with a whoosh of breath as I struggle to speak, lost in the friction of his girth and teetering on the brink of collapse. I'm so slick, arousal slips from my pussy and douses my thighs with every plunge.

He quickly notices and slips his hand between us, gathering my juices and rubbing them onto my clit. He teases me, flicking my swollen nub in time with every thrust of his pistoning cock, and pulls my strings like a marionette.

"I thought I lost you, baby. I thought you ran away." He strokes harder, lashing my clit in tiny circles and flexing his hips, pumping faster, coming at me from every angle and beating my pussy into submission.

"Never. I'm yours," I breathe the words, each one truer now than ever before. "I belong to my daddy."

"I'm going to come inside you, little girl. I'm going to fill your cunt with everything I've got and then watch it slide out. Is that what you want?" He's not really asking. He just wants me to beg like the dirty girl I've become—the one he's created.

"Yes! Give me all your cum, Daddy. I want it. I need it." I fall forward onto my elbows and prop my ass higher, improving his angle and offering my pussy as tribute.

His muscles tense, stiffening as his thrusts slow and his breathing labors.

I love this part. I love knowing I can turn him on, make him lose control, and climax inside me. I want to be the only one who ever makes him feel this way. I live to feel him plunging inside me, rocking, rocking, growing bigger with every thrust until the friction is too much to bear. So, I don't bear it—I release everything inside me, every thought, every prayer emerges in a shuddering scream, and we fall together as one. I've been alone all my life and don't feel alone anymore. He's the only man I'll ever love, and there's no going back for me.

"Only mine. Always mine," he pants and pulls me into his arms. His lips find mine, and I relish this quiet moment after our storm when all that's left is love.

"Marry me, baby. Make me your husband," he says with a shy smile, and steals the rest of my heart.

"Yes, Daddy."

CHAPTER 15

EPILOGUE SIX YEARS LATER
OLIVER

"Back off! Mr. Warbrick is a respectable businessman, a gentleman, and a captain of industry. He's a philanthropist with a heart of gold who helps children in need throughout New York. How about you take a look at the press release, study it, and get back to us with some real questions." Annika holds her arms like a referee and guides Grace and me through a throng of legitimate reporters and paparazzi, fielding questions and threatening to confiscate cameras. She may be my wife, but she's also the head of my public relations team and an all-around shark with the press.

God, I fucking love to watch her work.

My girl took five years to graduate because I knocked her up during her freshman year at NYU, but she never gave up and pushed through until she got that diploma. Like I promised, she interned every summer and hit the ground running as soon as she was done. She takes her job seriously, no funny business during company hours. But occasionally, she gives me a pass and schedules a long lunch in my office with no food involved.

I understand her ambition. I have plenty of my own. She could have had an easy life and lived like a lady of leisure without a care in the world, with my money at her disposal. But that isn't her style. At first, she said she had something to prove to herself and me. She knows what it's like to struggle and live a precarious life at the mercy of others, and she's terrified of falling back into that cycle.

I assure her there is nothing to worry about. I'll never leave her, and be damned if I ever let her walk away.

After all, what's a daddy without his little girl?

Camera flashes and unhinged shouting follows us into the lobby. This is my brother's fault. The world-class dick has gotten in trouble again. After what happened with Anni at the opera, I threatened to press charges if he didn't return to whatever rock he crawled out from under. He disappeared for a while, stayed under the radar for a couple of years, then re-emerged last year in the company of an heiress.

It was his dream come true. A woman with money to fund the life of leisure he craves. He became the boy toy, the sugar baby to a woman with almost as much money as me. Almost.

But Phillip can never leave well enough alone.

Six months in, he grew tired of being a one-woman man and got caught with his pants down. The women in his life have always let him get away with murder, so he grossly underestimated the wrath of a woman scorned. Either she discovered he'd been stealing, or forged documents to implicate him for grand larceny. The jury is still out on that —literally.

Since the woman's legal team subpoenaed me as a hostile witness, Anni's been working her magic to control the damage. No one wants to be associated with a gigolo and thief—even if he is my brother.

"All right! That's enough!" My little girl lifts her arms and makes a circular motion, signaling security to clear the area. "You people are now trespassing on private property. Clear it out or suffer the consequences."

Someone shouts, proclaiming their rights under the First Amendment, but Anni won't be swayed. She knows what she's doing. She points him out in the crowd and summons the biggest, burliest guard to throw him out first.

"Come on, sweetheart. Let them take care of it." I call her to my side and usher her toward the elevator. Grace hangs back and deals with the crowd, ensuring everyone exits the building without making a mess. Annika straightens her suit and enters my code, finally exhaling a sigh of relief when the car ascends.

I sidle next to her and stare longingly, beaming with pride at my little girl, my wife and mother to our son, Alex, the most rambunctious five-year-old boy in Manhattan. There's nothing she can't do.

"Did you mean it?" I ask a cryptic question expecting her to understand. She always does.

"To call you a gentleman?" She fluffs her hair and does a horrible job of disguising her smile. "You have your moments."

"Are you joining me for lunch?" I take hold of her hand and bring it to my lips.

"It's 10:00 in the morning, Oliver."

"What did you call me?" I crowd her into a corner, unsatisfied with her reply. "Is that the way you address your daddy?" I'm breaking the rules, but we're technically alone, and I need an outlet after the stress of Phillip's trial.

She pouts and steps forward, tapping the button to halt the car. I stare, confused, wondering why we shouldn't head straight to my office. "You told me to tell you when I was ready for another baby."

I nod, reach for my collar, and unfasten my tie before she finishes her announcement. "Are you?"

Annika unbuttons her blouse and kicks off her pumps. "Your little girl is ready to make her daddy a real daddy...

again." She corrects herself with a grin, bends forward, and slides off her panties.

"Say no more." I unbuckle my belt, unzip my slacks, and whip out my always-hard cock. "Bring it on, little girl. Daddy is going to fuck another baby into that sweet pussy before the end of the day."

Annika's eyes grow as wide as saucers. She stares at my cock, looks to the ceiling then brings her eyes back to me. "Holy shit, Oliver. There are cameras in here."

My face grows hot. I immediately stash my dick and throw my jacket over Anni's tits, furious that some jackass enjoyed the view too much. I tap the button holding us still, then press the button to go down. "I've waited five years for the green light and there's no way I'm giving you time to change your mind. You're not getting out of this, baby girl. Alex gets home from kindergarten in six hours. I've got a job to do and just like you, I take my fucking work seriously. Let's go home."

THANKS FOR READING!

ABOUT THE AUTHOR

Matilda is a Texas girl in love with a Philly boy who loves to write dirty books about two people who trip into love and fumble their way into a Filthy, Funny, Happily Ever After.

I live in Austin, with my husband, two crazy Chihuahuas and an even crazier cat. And I spend most of my day writing dirty romance books about older men who fall in love with younger women and make fools of themselves trying to win their hearts.

I like my hero to be successful, sweet, suave, sophisticated and kind--- and then I want him to lose all his composure and game when he meets the heroine. I want him to turn into a bumbling idiot when he spots the girl of his dreams and revert to a teenage boy in a man's body trying to win her.

I like my heroines to be witty, intelligent, and unshake-able---who could do just as well without a man—until the hero convinces her otherwise.

I write A LOT OF AGE GAP--because I LOVE AGE GAP ROMANCE. I've got no other excuse for it.

No matter what kind of story it is, my ladies are ADORED, and my endings are always Happily EVER AFTER, not HFN.

To receive a free ebook, join Matilda Martel's newsletter.

Please head to my website to learn what's in the final stages and will be coming out soon!

ALSO BY MATILDA MARTEL

DO YOU LOVE STEAMY AGE GAP ROMANCE?

Those are my favorites.

If you like them as much as me,

you might like these titles:

Love in War

Duplicity

Mile High Senator

Green-Eyed Monster

My Second Chance

Summer Storm

Stalked by my Roommate

We'll Always Have Paris

Vanished in Manhattan

Takeover

Blind Faith

Happenstance

Simmering for the Sous Chef

Off the Market

Blindsided

Get Your Kicks

The Pastor

In Praise of Older Men

My Heart's Desire

Maestro

Gilded Cage

Love Match

Play Right

The Man I Love

Bad Boss

Clever Girl

Chasing Zoe

The Good Girl

My Ward

Do you love Billionaire Romances?

Try these titles:

Takeover

Filthy Rich

Filthy Love

Blindsided

Gilded Cage

Magic Man

Hostile Takeover

There She Goes

Agreeably Arranged

Bad Boy

Off the Market

Snowed in with the Boss

Do you love Friends to Lovers?

Shut Up & Kiss Me

Unsuitable

Lucky Man

Marry Me

Summer Storm

Do you love Mafia Romances?

Check out my BROOKLYN BAD BOYS and

CRIMINALLY IN LOVE

Love Interrupted

Love Unleashed

Love Revealed

And

Vanished in Manhattan

Secret Weapon

And

Duplicity

BAD BOYS TURNED GOOD?

Check out SCOUNDRELS IN LOVE

Bad Professor

Bad Boss

Bad Boy

PHILLY BOYS FIND LOVE IN LOVE BITES

Love Hate

Love Nest

Love Match

And many more!

Thanks for reading and I hope you come back again!

www.ingramcontent.com/pod-product-compliance
Lightning Source LLC
Chambersburg PA
CBHW060445160726

47992CB00003B/1081

9798215992869